Bernd Curvt
Psalms 40:1-3

On The Trail

CHRISTIAN COWBOY POEMS AND PROVERBS

BRAD CURTIS

authorHOUSE®

AuthorHouse™
1663 Liberty Drive
Bloomington, IN 47403
www.authorhouse.com
Phone: 1-800-839-8640

First published by AuthorHouse   10/27/2010

ISBN: 978-1-4520-9003-0 (sc)
ISBN: 978-1-4520-9007-8 (hc)
ISBN: 978-1-4520-9008-5 (e)

Library of Congress Control Number: 2010915708

Printed in the United States of America

This book is printed on acid-free paper.

Certain stock imagery © Thinkstock.

Dedication

Over the years there have been many people in my life who have supported me through many trials. The one person who has stood with me when I was face down in the dirt and when I was riding high in the saddle is my wife Janet. It has been because of her love and support that I have been able to preach in churches all over Arkansas, attend Bible college, serve as a pastor, study, write—the list could go on forever. Jesus and Janet have been with me through it all and are my everything!

David Gaither of Bedford, Virginia, picked me up at a rodeo on June 26, 1986, and told me about Christ. He did not tell me about a church or denomination, just Jesus. If the Lord had not put this man in my life, I would not be here today. I was raised in the South where there is a church on every corner, and it was not until I was twenty-two that someone shared Christ with me. I will never forget the time I spent with him and his family and what it meant to me.

Jerry Johnson of Harrison, Arkansas, has played such a key role in my life and has really never known it. He is the one Christian and friend whom I turned to more than anyone else. When I became a Christian, many of my "friends" deserted me. I would call Jerry almost every week just to talk. He has no idea what those conversations meant to me and the trouble they kept me out of. One of the greatest things God did for me was put this man in my life so I would have someone just to talk to during times of struggle.

Jim Moore of Conway, Arkansas, is the man who had a great influence on me early in my walk. In 1987 he started a cowboy church Bible study. He is the one who taught me about the word of God, prayer, and God's love for me. Every Sunday night in that little building was an experience, to say the least.

Stan Stewart of Guy, Arkansas, has been a friend for many years; we first met at a rodeo at Roy Lee's in Mt. Vernon, Arkansas, in 1979 or 1980. A lot of things have changed in the past thirty years, and we both have seen good times and bad. Stan is the reason I joined my first church, and he was the best man in my wedding and the first person I called when my mom passed away. It is through our friendship that I realized that the Lord did not want to change who I was but rather what I was. This has greatly influenced my approach to ministry.

Brother Ken Jordan of Friendship Baptist Church in Conway, Arkansas, became my pastor in 1997. As far as my ministry, there has not been any greater influence than Brother Ken. He encouraged me to attend Bible college, gave me opportunities to preach, and gave me advice that can only come from years of experience. I still remember standing in the church parking lot and being taught by him how to tie a tie. He has been a great pastor and friend. The greatest thing he has done for me is that he saw in me things that others did not. He did not allow me to sit in a pew and waste what God had given me.

As you read these poems, you will see that my dad has also been a great influence in my life. He is the best man I have ever known, and I wish I were more like him. There was nothing greater as a young man than spending time with my father. He never pushed me to ride bucking horses but was more than willing to help me. We spent a lot of time together on horses and going to rodeos. Since I became a pastor, I have found no greater joy than knowing that he is a Christian and active in his church. My dad is my father, friend, and hero. Amen.

Last but not least, I want to thank the many friends who took care of me when I was on the rodeo trail. The list is too long to provide here, but you know who you are. Thanks to those who gave me a place to sleep, food to eat, and money for my fees at times when I was down and to those who were just good friends. Many years have passed, but I still remember being on the rodeo trail.

Contents

FOREWORD

Being a pastor of a cowboy church myself, I have found that one struggle often faced is finding material that cowboys and cowgirls can relate to, something that speaks our language but also has a spiritual aspect. This book of cowboy poetry that Brad has written is just that, a book that speaks the cowboy/cowgirl language and has the spiritual viewpoint. The book will also provide inspiration to anyone who has dreamed of being a cowboy/cowgirl or just enjoys the western heritage lifestyle.

Because Brad has had a variety of life experiences, he understands the heart of the western heritage culture; and now serving as a pastor of a cowboy church, he understands both sides of the fence. This book of cowboy poetry will be a point of inspiration to one and all who read it. Happy trails.

Bill Howse
Pastor, Bar None Cowboy Church
Mountain Home, AR

I met Brad Curtis in a classroom setting a number of years ago. If you know Brad at all, you know this was an unusual setting for anyone to meet Brad. Academic pursuits had not been a priority for him, but God has a way of changing our priorities. That first class was a struggle for Brad for a lot of reasons, but he persevered and made it through. His journey from that point to now has not been easy. When God begins the process of transforming our lives, He already knows what He wants us to be and the things He wants us to do. Consequently, He is not really interested in our input. What He desires from us is our obedience. I believe that lesson is one that Brad has learned through the years. The character trait that I believe most defines Brad is dogged determination. He sticks to whatever he believes he is called to do. That determination to preach the word of God anywhere God would allow him to preach has opened the door for this project. In the pages of this book you will find the gospel of Jesus Christ presented through the eyes of a cowboy. The unique experiences of the cowboy lifestyle provide the backdrop for a powerful presentation of the truths in scripture. As you read what Brad has written and you find yourself drifting off into the world he creates with his words, I believe you will be gripped by the invitation of Jesus to put your faith in Him. If there is one thing that characterizes the lifestyle of a cowboy, it is dogged determination. What you will experience in these pages is the dogged determination of the Lord Jesus Christ to touch your soul. Enjoy!

Marty Watson
Pastor, Baring Cross Baptist Church
Sherwood, AR

PREFACE

There are two ways to be on the trail: sitting high in the saddle while taking in God's creation, or lying face down in the dirt unconscious. Either way, you're on the trail; one is just more enjoyable. Deuteronomy 5:32 says, "Ye shall observe to do therefore as the LORD your God hath commanded you: ye shall not turn aside to the right hand or to the left."

I spent fourteen years riding bareback horses and competing in rodeos all across this nation. I have had the opportunity to ride in thirty-six states and Canada. Although I never "made it big," it was not due to lack of effort or even talent; bad luck, bad decisions, and bad habits kept me from reaching many of my goals. However, it was at a rodeo that I came to know Christ.

It is through those years of traveling up and down the road that have influenced me as a Christian and pastor. Relating the Bible to those in a western-rodeo culture can be done only by someone who has been there. I have not only the T-shirt to prove it, but many scars as well.

As the pastor of Mountain Top Cowboy Church, I have discovered that there is little material designed specifically for cowboy churches. In October 2009, I broke my leg while competing at a forty-and-over bull-riding competition and required surgery. During my recovery, I started writing poems. As I wrote, I began to relate the poems to scripture and discovered after sharing them with my church that they could be a useful tool in cowboy churches and ministries and to others in the western culture.

OVER THE EDGE

I pulled up on the reins,
Slid him to a stop,
Sat back in the saddle,
Looking at a long, hard drop

Beads of sweat rose up
Beneath my hat's brim
Heart pounding
There at the valley rim

My bay shook beneath me,
As if to get my attention
Or maybe to relax and
Release some tension

Then he turned his head,
Seemed to look at me
Maybe to question
The challenge—did I see?

I looked all around
Just two trails to the other side
The choice seemed quite easy
Knowing the bay that I did ride

One trail around the rim
Was narrow and quite long
The other over the edge—
There was a lot that could go wrong

If I chose the narrow way
It would be a long trip
However, over the edge,
Half the distance I could skip

Wanting to take the shortcut,

I picked a spot to go over
This should not be that hard
For one who is a drover

The first step over the edge
My little bay did not want to make
Had to give him the spurs,
A gouge and a rake

So he took me over,
Headed down valley wall
Not much room for error
He seemed to be at a crawl

With every step
I just gave my bay his head
He knew where we were;
Sure-footed, well bred

Now rocks and dirt
Slid beneath my bay
He had brought me this far
Without even a sway

But about halfway down
I knew I had chosen wrong
It was steeper than I thought
Though my bay was strong

We were now in some brush
It hid the rocky trail
For the first time,
My bay felt a bit frail

When he slipped the first time,
I cursed and gasped for air
Then the second time,
I finally questioned why we were there

Now at that point
There was no turning back
The sun was going down,
The valley growing black

Then came the point
My bay drew to a halt
He knew what was ahead, and
We both knew who was at fault

I grabbed the horn,
With my split reins, I did whip
It was then my bay stumbled
This was the last slip

As my bay fell,
My mind began to race
I knew death was there
In darkened valley place

He rolled over me,
Then slid down the valley wall
Before I quit rolling,
His name I began to call

There on the valley floor,
I found my bay-horse friend
His eyes had that look
His life was near its end

He then looked up at me,
Not to blame ... maybe to say good-bye
There in that dark valley
I watched my friend die

As I gathered my things,
Saddle, tack, and gear,
I headed out of the valley
Looking back with a tear

As I stumbled walking,
There in that dark place
I came to a truth—
One I had to face

I was here in this valley
Because I did not choose the narrow way
Trying to take a shortcut
Had led me astray

The trail I chose
Was a costly one
Here in this dark valley,
No light from the sun

The trail over the edge
Not only affected me this day
But the choice to go that route
Took the life of my bay

Wandering there in dark,
I had to lighten the load
Saddle and tack were now lost
As my pace had slowed

As a new day broke,
I wandered the valley
My mind was spinning
The cost I did tally

Broken would not describe
How this cowboy felt
The hand that I had
Was one I had dealt

Lost, hungry, and thirsty,
Having lost my best friend,
The valley had almost gotten me
Could this be my end?

As I stumbled
In the valley dark and deep,
I encountered a shepherd
However, he had no sheep

Now this ol' cowboy
Was humbled to say the least
This shepherd not only showed me the way,
He prepared me a feast

I then had to ask
The shepherd about his flock
The answer that was given,
My life it did rock

He said, Cowboy
If you'll bow and pray,
You will be in my flock and
I'll show you the narrow way

I now had another choice
To follow and be led
Or stay there in the valley,
The Valley of the Dead

So it was there in the valley
With walls dark and steep
That this broken cowboy
Became a Shepherd's sheep

Matthew 14:28–30

DEATH IN THE DESERT

I had been riding hard
Determined not to look behind
Afraid of what was coming
No safety could I find

Asking a lot
From my stolen steed
There among the sand
And tumbling weed

I ran him into the ground
Stepped off and began to run
The one that pursued me
Knew all that I had done

My pursuer
No longer could I see
He was still back there
Never to let me be

With the heat beating down
Would this be the day
That he would catch me
And the price I would have to pay?

Now in the desert
Death upon my face
No life around
Here in the desolate place

Falling face down
Choking on the sand
Shadows circling around me
The time was at hand

It was then he caught me

Time to pay for my mistake
My pursuer was about to strike
The old deadly snake

Just then he rode up
A cowboy like I had never seen
Riding on a white horse
That was muscled-up and lean

Dressed in a robe
Long hair and sandals on his feet
With the look of a king
I no longer felt the heat

As he stepped off
He crushed the snake's head
Then said, Cowboy, get up
Your pursuer is defeated and dead

As I got up
No longer gasping for air
I had to ask this cowboy
What had brought him there

I am here
To show you love
Not only from me
But from my father above

He then got his canteen and said,
Drink and you will never thirst
Drank of his water
Thought I would burst

It seemed to never empty
Where did he get this canteen?
Always full of water
Fresh, cool, and clean

Then from his saddlebags
He pulled out a loaf of bread
Not offering me crumbs
But a feast I was fed

He then told me
Of all my crimes
The ones I had committed
Oh so many times

It was then
He looked in my eyes
Told me he had a gift
Not an earned prize

Then he asked
If I would believe
He said he offered redemption
It was mine to receive

Falling to my knees humbled
Tears falling to the sand
He reached out and touched me
With his scarred hands

As I stood up
Feeling like a new man
This strange cowboy
Told me he had for me a plan

He said, Cowboy
Go tell others about me
You will be my witness
From sea to sea

It was then I noticed
Two more white horses at his side
One was a pack horse
The other was to ride

He told me their names
Mercy and Grace
He had brought them for me
To ride out of the deadly place

As I rode out of the valley
Riding Grace who he'd put me on
Followed by Mercy
I knew my sin was gone

Now traveling the land
To tell about the one from above
The one who did not come to condemn
But to show this cowboy love

John 3:17

BACK AT THE RANCH

He had been a fisherman
Sailed the high seas
One day at port
A cowboy said, Follow me

Ol' Pete went along
Asking questions all the way
The cowboy told him,
You'll be my foreman one day

This was no ordinary cowboy
He was not from the West
His cattle were all strays
But his horses were the best

His crew was a sight to see
None would be called a top hand
But they listened to the Boss
All were riding for the brand

He showed them how to rope a stray
And how to dehorn
When they took the brand
It was like being reborn

But the other ranchers
Did not like the Boss
Every stray he gathered up
They counted as loss

The Boss told the crew,
They will destroy my spread
But no need to worry
You just keep the herd fed

Ol' Pete spoke up

Letting everyone know,
I'd die for you, Boss
By morning he was eatin' crow

Then a lynch mob showed up
Dragged the Boss into town
His cowboy hat was replaced
With a thorny crown

There in the town square
For everyone to see
Between two crooks
They hung him from a tree

The crew headed to the ranch
Talking along the way
Pete said, I've tried cowboying
I'm going back to fishing today

John 21:3

HONESTY IS NOT THE ACCEPTED POLICY

The year was 1985,
I was entered in a bucking horse sell
The place was Tulsa, Oklahoma
Here my story I have to tell

As I approached him,
I was waiting on the lie
Most stock contractors do it,
No matter if they are good guys

Not really expecting the truth,
I have to admit
I thought I would ask,
Just to see what I would get

Then something happened
That sticks with me to this day
When I asked about my bronc
This is what he had to say

He started by saying,
Son, she's pretty bad
Never knew anyone to draw her
Who was really glad

She's that little sorrel,
The one with three white socks
To be honest,
She really fights the box

If you get out on her,
My words I will not mince
She will circle to the left,
Then she will hit the fence

Now if you're still with her,
She'll drop her head and swoop right
After that we're not sure,
No one's lasted that long in the fight

My head dropped in self-pity,
Thinking on what I had learned
I was in need of good news
When would it be my turn?

I headed to my truck
To grab my cowboy gear
He yelled out with a laugh
So all around could hear

He said, I forgot to tell you,
As I walked out of sight
About that little mare,
Watch her—she really likes to bite

There at my truck,
Thinking about my task
If I did not want the truth,
Well, I guess I shouldn't have asked

Surely it couldn't be that bad,
At least that's what I thought
As I headed to the arena
To spur the bronc he'd brought

They ran her in the chute
She began to start her fight
If I were to be honest,
She was a scary sight

One of my buddies there
Tried to get a neck rope on her
I had not told him what I'd learned
From this little bronc's owner

That's when she bit him
On his left shoulder
As it turned out,
The rope wouldn't hold her

They then motioned to me
To get my riggin' on this nightmare
This was the baddest bronc I'd encountered,
To that, I would swear

After quite a battle
And suggestions from every so-called hand
I was easing my way into the chute
It was then they fired up the band

Every cowboy scattered
Like a covey of quail
She was plum evil
From mane to tail

As she flipped over and mashed me
Into the back of the chute
I started thinking about a new job,
One where I could wear a tie and suit

It was then one of my buddies
Pushed my hat down tight
He said, Cowboy up
Spur this bronc tonight

That's when I got that feeling,
My chest began to swell
She's the one that had drawn badly
Here at this buckin' horse sell

I finally got mounted
Time to see what else she could do
All that the contractor told me
Simply could not be true

They threw the gate open,
This mare, she came apart
The next thing that happened
Almost broke my heart

She circled to the left,
Then she hit the fence
My mind was still spinning
None of this made any sense

She was doing …
Well, what the stock contractor said
To be honest,
I thought he was messing with my head

It was then she ducked right
I spurred over her neck
What happened next can only be described
As a wild cowboy wreck

When it was all over,
My body was blue and red
As for my chaps and shirt,
They were in need of needle and thread

There I was in the arena,
In a bloody torn-up pile
The contractor could be heard laughing
At least for a country mile

All eyes were on me
There was no place for me to hide
Still in shock and disbelief
I had met a stock contractor who hadn't lied

As I limped out of the arena,
All would have to agree
I had been humbled by this bronc
For all there to see

The lesson that I learned that night,
Years ago in my youth
Is often we ask questions
Not willing to hear the truth

So, cowboy, when you're on bended knee
And crying out to the Lord
Be prepared for him to tell you the truth,
And it shouldn't be ignored

    John 15:7

THE DRIVE

The day had been long and hard
As we pushed the herd
Horse and cowboy tired
Both needed to be spurred

At the entrance of the valley
I was riding drag
Dust thick and heavy
Enough to make you gag

Pulled up on the reins
As I did hesitate
Heading into the valley
Seemed dark and late

The herd was spooked
In this shadowy place
I was a bit worried
For the worst I did brace

Alone, my mind began to wander
Every shadow seemed to creep
Something hiding behind the rocks
In the valley dark and deep

Why did we come to this valley
There had to be a better trail
Danger all around
Death I could smell

The shadows did move
As they caught my eye
Here in this valley
I would surely die

I kept pushing forward
In this valley place
Watching every shadow
Not knowing what I'd face

As I passed by
Every shadow on the ground
Seemed like I had won a victory
Courage had been found

I began to realize
The trail boss was up ahead
Looking out for the herd
In the valley he had led

Then my mind was eased
He'd been this way before
The valley was not that long
This trail had much more

Word was sent back
We were near the valley's end
What was on the other side
My mind couldn't comprehend

As I rode out of the valley
Not losing one cow or steer
Into a green pasture
With a creek calm and clear

The trail boss rode up
With a smile on his face
Said, If we had ridden around the valley
We would have missed this glorious place

The herd began to graze
The calm water they did drink
I sat there with peace
Now I had time to think

It was then I understood
I would follow the trail boss
If I'd have gone my way
All would be counted as lost

He knew the way
All that was up ahead
The next valley I rode through
I would not dread

For the drive was not over
Many miles of trail ahead
Trail boss out in front
Herd and cowboys being led

Well mounted was the trail boss
With catch rope in hand
Led us through the valley
Headed to the promised land

He had bought and paid for
Every critter on this drive
It was because of him
I came through the valley alive

Psalm 23

THE CLOSING OF THE TRIPLE 6 SALOON

We had heard of his work
It spread across the land
He could clean up a town
Always took a stand

He rode the high country
On his father's spread
Lived in a mansion
Not some ol' cowboy shed

So we sent word
Come and save our town
Filled with death and violence
Is all that is found

The day he arrived
All felt like fools
He came riding in
On a borrowed mule

Surely this couldn't be
The man we had sent for
He was not ready for a fight
Much less a mighty war

Then it was noticed
Nothing was strapped to his side
We had called for protection
How could he provide?

Now he rode up
Stepped off that sorry mule
Said, I am here to forgive
And teach a golden rule

With that he strolled in
To the Triple 6 saloon
There he was met
By a Colt Dragoon

He never flinched a muscle
Or raised his voice
He said simply, Cowboys,
Today make a choice

Follow me this day
Ride for my dad and I
Or stay here in the Triple 6
Believing a hellish lie

What I have to offer
Is not of this earth
An abundant life
My life is what it's worth

The pistol was holstered
Triple 6 cleared out
All stared at him
No one had any doubt

There they all stood
In the middle of the street
As he explained
You will no longer feel the heat

Where we are headed
Is my father's place
The trail we will take
Is the one called grace

The owner of the Triple 6
Came running out
His eyes full of fire
Thinking he had clout

He said, You men
What do you crave?
I can give it to you
If you'll be my slave

Fisher Pete spoke up
Not to be bold and brash
Said, Clear away
Or we will surely clash

In the Triple 6
We will no longer patronize
Going to the high country
To grow strong and wise

Then the new sheriff
Said, Red Lou
You're a thief and a liar
These men don't belong to you

Red Lou knew he was defeated
As he dropped his head
Returning to the Triple 6
The place was truly dead

The sheriff said, Boys
We have work to do today
On the way to my father's ranch
We'll look for those gone astray

As the sheriff and his posse
Rode out of sight
We realized he had won the battle
Without an earthly fight

The Triple 6 was closed
By a sheriff from above
His badge was forgiveness
Pistols replaced by love

John 10:10

THE BAR-SIN RANCH

I was a young cowboy
With a lot to learn
How to get my dally
To get one to turn

As for riding skills
Those I did lack
Spent more time on the ground
Lying on my back

To say I had been a rounder
That would come up short
A hard-riding cowboy
You know the sort

When in town
Would end up on the floor
The only way out
Crawling under a swing door

So when I was hired on
To be a ranch hand
Nowhere could a sorrier cowboy
Be found across this land

The ramrod gave me a horse
His name was Ol' Gray
Said he was a good horse
Would not go astray

He began to teach me
What I needed to know
When to push hard
Times I needed to go slow

As I made mistakes
He did not dock my pay
With words of wisdom
He pointed out the errors of my ways

There were those times
He would send me to town
I would have to ride past that place
The one that had pulled me down

With a reminder
He would always say
You are now part of Bar-Sin
Don't go astray

Upon return
He would never ask
Knowing I had victory
Had carried out my task

So then the day came
To move the herd out
The trail boss rode up
Said he had a route

As the low man
I'd be riding drag
Ramrod rode up
And gave me a new wild rag

The days were long
On a dry dusty trail
The sun beat down
This was cowboy hell

But the worst day
Was better than my past
The Bar-Sin had given me
Something that would last

My skills as a cowboy
They grew every day
Ramrod would ride up
Ask about me and Ol' Gray

Would always say thanks
For the horse I ride
And for the ramrod
My life he did guide

Every day on the trail
Was better than the one before
Now I had purpose
No crawling on the floor

Sitting around at night
There by the campfire
Listening to cowboy stories
Gave me more desire

Before sunrise
I saddled Ol' Gray
Checked all my tack
Another cowboy day

Trail boss and owner
Rode out before the rest
Ramrod and outriders
We were pushing northwest

This day started
Like the ones before
Riding drag, eating dust
Not knowing what was in store

As we moved the herd
Into a desert place
The wind picked up
Our tracks it did erase

I pulled my wild rag up
For all the dust
Could barely see the herd
The wind began to gust

This was my first drive
Would it be my last?
My eyes were stinging
As the sand began to blast

The outriders fell back
To see if I was there
All now choking
As the dust filled the air

We all began to question
Why we were on this drive
Did not see a way
To come out of this storm alive

It was then
The ramrod rode back
The sun was covered
The sky growing black

He then asked the outriders
If the herd they could see
Then he wiped his face
Turning to me

He said, Young cowboy
You now ride for the Bar-Sin
As for this herd
We will bring them in

For this storm
Is part of the job
So keep pushing on
Behind this longhorn mob

With that he explained,
My father owns this herd
If you need assurance
I can send him word

In a matter of seconds
A rider came riding in
Whispered to the ramrod
He sat there with a grin

He said, I have a message
I want all to hear
As he spoke
His words were strong and clear

He said, I own the cattle
On a thousand hills
He then lifted his hand
And said, Peace, be still

The wind did cease
No dust blowing around
I dropped my head in shame
Looking toward the ground

The ramrod rode over
Said, This ain't my first drive
Every cowboy that is with me
I assure will survive

He said, You have my father
Out front every day
I am riding with you
And you're riding Ol' Gray

With that he added,
Cowboy, lift your chin
Keep pushing forward
You're riding for the Bar-Sin

Mark 4:35–5:1

THREE DAYS' RIDE

Headed for the ranch
A three days' ride
The sun and stars
A cowboy's guide

A storm arose
Lost my way
Now it was dark
End of the day

Alone in camp
Fire put out by rain
In the darkness
Cold and in pain

A big cat circling
One I had never seen
Seeking to devour
His senses keen

Horse was spooked
Ears pinned back
Pawing the earth
Awaiting attack

My knife was dull
Powder was not dry
Darkness was broken
Lightning in the sky

Hunger and thirst
Now consumed my soul
Wet and shivering
On my bedroll

Saddlebags were empty
Canteen was dry
Cat still circling
Surely I would die

Hour passed
A new day's start
Looking around
Now fear in my heart

I had camped by a grave
That stormy night
Nothing living here
A ghostly sight

Jumped to my feet
Grabbed my gear
Saddled up
That cat I could hear

Heart a-racing
My pony broke free
No way to escape
Death it would be

That cat came charging
Fire in his eyes
Thunder exploded
Rumbling sky

My legs trembling
Heart started quaking
That grave opened up
The ground was shaking

A man stepped out
Nothing was said
The earth was still
That cat dropped dead

I dropped to my knees
Said, Thank you, sir
Nothing could be heard
But my trembling spur

My pony returned
Time to head home
A clear trail ahead
Not having to roam

That's when he said,
Cowboy, you've found the way
Because of my journey
And this third day

That cat is defeated
You have a new life
Follow the Son
And sharpen your knife

Tell other cowboys
About this trail
Follow the Son to heaven
Or that big cat into hell

Proverbs 27:17

RUSTLERS REDEEMED

He rode up on 'em
Rustling his herd
Caught 'em red-handed
His anger was stirred

That's my herd
All carry my brand
Release them now
That's a command

The rustlers took note
Of his mighty steed
Pure white
Registered indeed

One spoke up,
Mister, I like your horse
Think I'll take him
No pay, of course

Standing in the saddle
With eyes like a flame
Dressed in all white
Never gave his name

He spoke soft at first,
Dad gave me this stud
Sent me for his herd
Paid for it in blood

His voice now stern
Like a rolling river
The herd was on the move
Earth began to quiver

As they looked at him
The sun grew bright
His gold buckle
Shining in the light

Said, Boys, dismount
Turn from your wicked way
Rustling has a price
A rope is its pay

Come work for me
I own a large spread
Always green grass
Never dry or dead

They dropped to their knees
He reached out his hand
Now part of his herd
Carrying the Three Cross brand

You were rustlers
But I know the judge
Trust me, boys
He doesn't hold a grudge

Looking down on them
Hand on a two-edged sword
Said, My name is Jesus
You now call me Lord

Revelation 1:10–18

THE FALLEN ROUND UP

We hired on to gather up strays
Knew where to look due to our past ways

The Boss said, Get 'em, bring 'em all in
They're hiding out where you've once been

Take what you need to round them up
I had a good horse and blue heeler pup

Headed out early, before sunrise
To beat the brush under heavenly skies

We jumped one up that was asleep
In a canyon with walls high and steep

In that valley full of grit and sand
At the end of his rope, he took the brand

We brought him back, the Boss was proud
The sound of the herd grew very loud

Now dehorned, given a shot
Time for him to grow in the feedlot

No longer a stray there in the herd
All the hands' spirits were moved and stirred

Time to head out to find other strays
Before the prairie is set ablaze

The ranch is huge, green grass and lots of space
Gathering more strays for this heavenly place

Luke 14:23

SILENT SPURS

Stories of old, from days of his youth
They seem like yesterday an' he swears they're the truth

Spurs don't jingle; his stirrups seem too high
Rope won't swing 'cause he's no longer spry

His old hat's stained from all the years
Of riding hard and brandin' steers

Hands like leather; they've held many a rein
A-bustin' broncs; he's now weathered in pain

His old boots are worn 'cause he's had them awhile
Never once been polished; they're cowboy style

Buckle's been tarnished over time
Won years ago while in his prime

His chaps are old and the leather's worn
From poppin' brush, cactus, and thorn

Saddle's no prize, cracked leather and tree
But it fits him well, good horsemen agree

Now he's here at the end of his trail
But his cow pony is sure 'nuff not for sale

Says, I'm a cowboy till my last day
Listen, young cowboys, to what I say

The Lord's retuning with a shout
I won't die; I'll just be turned out

In heaven's green pasture I will ride
With the good Lord riding by my side

2 Timothy 4:7

RIDING DOUBLE

We met up there on the trail
I was headed toward heaven, he, toward hell

I noticed he had the reins pulled tight
Headed down that trail in a devilish fight

As we passed each other, I was singing a hymn
He was crying out, My future is grim

His pony was black with a 666 brand
Mine was white, from a heavenly land

I said, Cowboy, where you're headed today
No need to go; your debt has been paid

His pony wouldn't stop; he was headin' down fast
That's when I said, Jesus will forgive your past

He said, This trail is all I know
I replied, You're not going to like what's down below

I pulled up and reached out a hand
Said, Cowboy, you better make a stand

Confess to the Lord, of your ways repent
Climb on my horse; he's heaven-sent

He cried out and jumped off ol' black
I picked him up and he rode on back

We began to sing, heading up the trail
Riding toward heaven instead of hell

Luke 15:7

THE PICK-UP MAN

I was entered, like so many times before
Never heard that bronc The Devil let out his hellish roar

I had that bronc for all the world to see
What I didn't know was that he really had ahold of me

Now as a bronc rider, I knew no fear
Trusting in myself and my cowboy gear

So when I was warned about my wild ride
Said, I'll spur him, with all my cowboy pride

Then life's gate came open, rank right out of the gate
I was in it to win, not knowing my fate

As the seconds passed, I kept waiting for the horn
After a while, I was wishing I hadn't been born

This ride was wild; my life would be the cost
Hung up to The Devil, I was surely lost

I tried with all my might to get set free
But that ol' bronc The Devil said, You belong to me

That's when it happened; he came riding in
Said, Cowboy, without me, you will never win

This pick-up man was from heaven, dressed all in white
To be honest, he was a welcomed sight

He called out, said, Cowboy, you can be set free
Turn loose of The Devil and grab ahold of me

As I reached out to him, his scarred hands held me tight
The Devil was a-bucking, wouldn't give me up without a fight

The pick-up man sat me down on life's arena floor
The announcer called out, Cowboy, you now have a perfect
score

Psalm 103:12

PROTECTOR

I was coming to the end of my rodeo career
Ridin' bulls was all I knew on life's grand frontier

For my last ride, I drew one from the eliminator pin
His name was Lucifer; we just called him ol' buckin' sin

He stood there in the chute calm as could be
As I warmed up my rope, he never took note of me

One of my buddies said, Watch him, he's a deceiver and a liar
That's when I noticed his hide seemed to feel like fire

They pulled my rope, I took my wrap, then I shook my head
That's when ol' Lucifer's eyes seemed to turn fire red

He blew high and came down hard, was a living hell
Turned back to the left, dropped me in the well

I was hung up and in a storm as my rope seemed to get tighter
That's when I heard three voices but saw only one bullfighter

He stepped in and put his life on the line
This man who came to save me would trade his life for mine

It was as if he didn't even touch my bull rope
All I saw on his jersey were the words love, faith, and hope

I was free from Lucifer, that ol' buckin' sin
As he continued to buck and spin

It was then I noticed the bullfighter on the arena floor
As that devilish bull did hook and gore

They carried him off as a tear came to my eye
The other bullfighter said, Don't worry, my Son will not die

He said, Cowboy, your life was spared today
If I were you, I'd kneel and pray

I dropped to my knees and called to Lord above
Said, I want to thank you for this bullfighter who showed me love

Then it happened, as they ran Lucifer through the out gate
He dropped dead in his tracks; no more buckin' hate

Then into the arena returned that rodeo clown
He said, I'm your savior, and Lucifer cannot keep me down

Luke 19:10

TRUE TREASURES

Some think it's just a gold buckle,
But a story it does tell
It cannot be bought
These are never for sale

Its cost was high
And value cannot be measured
All of those around him
Know that it is treasured

For the years he spent
Traveling across the land
Not an easy task
To get it in his hand

As one reflects
On the price that was paid
Many had helped,
Their support was displayed

So when you see it,
I pray you realize
There is much more to it
Than just a cowboy prize

The sacrifice was heavy,
His family paid the toll
They stood behind him
As he chased his goal

Many he grew up with
Did not understand
They thought he was a bum,
Traveling across the land

As for his body,
At the time he did not care
But with age,
The pain can be hard to bear

So now every day,
He humbly straps it on
The years have robbed his talent,
But the memories are never gone

Now he is fading,
Just part of the crowd
Wearing that gold buckle,
Wearing it, and wearing it proud

You see, in this world,
Many say they are a success
But my friend is a champion,
That gold buckle does profess

Yes, it may be from years ago,
The years of his youth
But when among cowboys,
We all know it tells the truth

And that truth is certain
As he wears it on display
There is no need for words,
He has a gold-buckle resume

But as great as it is,
That buckle he does wear
His greatest treasure
Came from a simple prayer

While that buckle
May be his cowboy resume
His greatest treasure is salvation,
And the price Jesus did pay

Now laying up treasures,
In heaven they do lay
More valuable than gold and silver
And they will never rust nor decay

Matthew 6:19–21

MY FAIR LADY

As the sun arose
The light did break
Sleep in my eyes
Barely awake

Put on my hat
Rolled out of bed
Then shirt, jeans, and boots
Cowboy, without being said

Open the door
To a new day
Thought for a moment,
I do this for pay

The smell of fresh rain
Was still in the air
Talked with the Lord
With a quick prayer

Out to the barn
Met by a good friend
I said, Good morning
To her needs I would tend

First came a meal
To give her might
Then brush and comb
Ah, what a lovely sight

Had to check her shoes
She had a good pair
Now for her wardrobe
Leather, she would wear

After getting dressed
She had to wait on me
What a beautiful sight
For all to see

She would be the object
Of the other cowboys' desire
It's a shame she has to go out
In the muck and the mire

But there she was
Fed, groomed, and dressed
I have to say,
Looking her best

So I took my partner
Out into the sun
Her ears perked up
She was ready to run

It was then I knew
I could attest
This old cowboy
Was truly blessed

I had a home and food
And a great job
A joy and peace
That no one could rob

I now had a friend
That was not shady
And most of all
I had My Fair Lady

GOOD HORSES, BAD COWBOY

He came to buy a cow pony,
Said he was a hand
Was heading out west to be a cowboy
And ride across the land

I had my reservations
As he pulled through the gate
Must have needed a watch,
He was an hour late

I asked if he'd gotten lost
Or had taken a wrong turn
The answer I got was, Nah
Well, he had a lot to learn

Informed him that on a ranch,
A man's word is all he has
Not knowing if he understood,
I had this to add

Time is like money,
Not much left of it to spare
If the boss says seven A.M.,
You need to be right there

He then got out of his truck,
Walked over without a word
The thought of him as a cowboy,
Well, was absolutely absurd

I looked down at his boots,
They had the new boot shine
They'd never seen a stirrup
This wasn't a good sign

As we headed to the barn,
It was as if he was afraid of the ground
Watching his every step
To avoid every mound

I said, Son, it won't kill you,
I do not mean to sass
But after all, pardner,
It's just water and grass

As we walked through the barn,
Questions he did ask
To keep from laughing
Was quite a task

I showed him a few good ones
That sure could work a cow
Good-looking horse flesh,
Ones that would raise a brow

Then we came to a stall,
It was here I got the fact
His knowledge of horses,
It was just a silly act

I knew as a cowboy
He would not fare too well
Pointing, he said, I want him,
The stud with black mane and tail

This cowboy had a problem,
He was in need of prayer
The stud he was looking at
Was a twenty-year-old mare

So I got out a saddle,
It was an awful sight
Watching him put it on
Told of a horrible plight

When it came time for bridle,
There was not much to be said
Bits went in pretty easy,
She didn't have a tooth in her head

I led her out of the barn
As he tiptoed through the "mud"
All the time he kept talking
About this good-looking stud

After I gave him a boost up,
I had to bite my lip
His knuckles were bone white,
Holding the horn with a death grip

Now forcing the reins in his hands
And then stepping back
Told him to just relax
And give him some slack

I let out a little chuckle
As they disappeared out of sight
I had things to do,
No more burning daylight

About an hour later,
I could hear on his return
This is the sorriest horse,
His voice loud and stern

I asked, What's the problem?
And to my dismay
He said he was not going to be a cowboy,
Not for board and pay

Then he informed me,
That is a sorry horse
Would not go where he wanted,
Could not stay the course

That's when I started the lesson,
Shall we call it cowboy school
There is but one teacher,
And there is really only one rule

First of all, I stated,
This is not a stud but a mare
She is dead broke
A child could ride her, I swear

Here is the problem,
One you cannot hide
You are the cowboy,
The leader and the guide

She will only respond
To the reins as you direct
If she does not go where you want,
It's due to your defect

You can put on boots and hat,
Take cowboy as your name
But the truth will be revealed in the end
He then dropped his head in shame

It was then I looked him in the eye
And asked something he did not expect,
Do you really want to be a cowboy?
Take a minute to reflect

He answered, Yes, I do,
Truly with all my heart
But to be honest,
I do not know where to start

It's then I told him,
Welcome, come on in and unpack
School is now open
To learn about horse and tack

When we are finished,
You'll be ready to head out west
And find joy
In our cowboy quest

You see, my cowboy friend,
I have a calling and a duty
To train young cowboys
And not to be judgmental or snooty

So give up the reins
And learn some new cowboy skills
And I'll tell you about the one
Who owns the cattle on a thousand hills

Matthew 28:18–20

INHERITANCE

There it hung in the tack room,
Old, tattered, and worn
Strung from the rafters
By its rope-scarred horn

Among the newer saddles,
It seemed a bit out of place
Some would've gotten rid of it
Simply to make more space

No hand-tooled designs,
No words did it garnish
As for the few conchos,
They were green with tarnish

The leather was cracked and dry
From many years of abuse
To a stranger who did not know better,
It would appear to be of no use

This old saddle was bought years ago
By a very young lad
He grew into a cowboy,
Then into my dad

As we would ride,
Many stories he would tell
How it had been used to gather cattle
And to break colts to sell

When I was a boy, I was so happy
To ride along by his side,
Dreaming of that great day
His saddle I would ride

While in my teens and in need of money,
He started buying colts for me to break
With dad's help and guidance,
That's all it did take

Then came the day I won my first saddle,
One that declared me the best
For years it just sat in the tack room
With dad's saddle and all the rest

With encouragement I convinced Dad
To ride the saddle I had won
Then one day while on a trail ride,
I noticed it was my trophy saddle he was riding on

When the ride was over,
He began to explain
The new saddle was easier to ride
And caused him no pain

With that he said the words I'd longed to hear,
Take my old saddle the next time we go
The feeling that filled my heart,
No one could really know

I rode that old, worn saddle
In what I'll call my best years
Just to sit in it
Would almost bring me to tears

Every memory of my youth
Revolved around the saddle that carried my dad
Working cattle, breaking colts, trail rides,
Ah, the fun we had

Then there was the day
I rode up along his side
Like so many times before,
Dad was my constant guide

Had a question for Dad,
Asked if with Christ he was on board
He told me not to worry
Because Jesus was his Lord

Then the years, as they will,
Caught up with my childhood idol
He no longer had any need
For a saddle and bridle

After a few years had passed,
He wanted to discuss his will
That's when I told my dad,
I think you know the deal

Of the land, house, and cattle, I wanted none
To tell the truth
My inheritance was to be the saddle,
The one of his youth

Some dream of gold and silver,
But that's not for me
My dream is worth more,
Made of leather and tree

Land and house may be lost,
And cattle can die
Things of great wealth
Are not where my desires lie

Memories and adventures,
In that saddle, many we did make
So what's my inheritance worth?
For it, nothing would I take
1 Peter 1:3–5

CAPTAIN COWBOY

As the rain falls,
Clouds do clap
Through the plains,
The herd leaves a muddy map

My slicker is covered with rain and mud
Feels as if it weighs a ton,
I'm just praying
That one doesn't break and run

This morning I felt young and fresh,
As the day did break
But cowboying in this toad-strangler
Is almost more than I can take

If I had wanted a job like this,
Wet and hard,
I would have learned to swim
And joined the coast guard

But I was not raised there
Around the ocean and reef
I'm here on the sea
Of grass and beef

As a boy I read about Ahab,
Who sought a great white whale
Now I'm about to drown
Pushing the herd on down the trail

Thoughts of getting a job in a store
Dance across my brain
No more working someone else's cows
In the cold and rain

I grab the horn
As my horse slips and stumbles
The clouds crash again
The sky shakes and rumbles

As the lightning flashes
Across the starless sky
I catch a glimpse of a little stray
Out of the corner of my eye

The sight of one separated from its mama,
That will get your attention
As the little lost calf just stands,
Shakin' and flinchin'

Through the dark and rain,
I ride over to the little feller
He sees me,
Begins to let out a beller

When I step off he just stands there with a look,
Please show me the way
So I gather him up
This is how a cowboy earns his pay

He is now drooped across my saddle
In front of me
As through the dark and cold
I strain to see

I now know I couldn't work in a store,
Dry and warm
This won't be the last lost one
There will be more

Through the crashing waves the great whale
Was sought out by a captain sailor
So I keep pushing on in the rain,
Looking for the next lost little feller

Acts 1:8

NEVER BE ANOTHER

Young and strong,
Set in his ways
Big dark eyes
That seemed to have a questionable gaze

Built like a god,
Muscled and lean
He was the best-looking horse
I'd ever seen

Buckskin in color,
Quarter horse bred
Put on this earth to work cattle
Does that have to be said?

Born on a feedlot
Stayed there until he was two years old
They didn't know what they had
Or he wouldn't have been sold

The smile on Dad's face
The first time he rode him told the story
It was as if he had died
And gone on to Glory

We named him Buck,
Out of lack of imagination
To Dad he was the greatest horse
In the entire nation

Working cows was a pleasure
For our horse named Buck
If one got by him,
It was just because of luck

I was twelve,
Been riding all my years
We were going riding
And gathering up some steers

My first time to ride Buck,
Thought like other horses he'd be the same
Learned pretty quick,
Moving cows on him wasn't a game
I'll tell you the truth
Buck wasn't a pleasure to ride
But when it came to cows,
He'd run over their sorry hides

He loved his job
Like no other you've seen
However, at times,
He could be downright mean

On more than one occasion,
He could not be caught
Made Dad question
Why he had been bought

Then there was the fact
He didn't like anything around his head
Ol' Buck also did not care much
For being tied up or being led

If something caught his eye
That was out of place
He would duck hard,
With strength and grace

For twenty years on our ranch,
He was the top ride
From him,
No cow could run or hide

But like all things,
Buck had to retire
He still loved pushing cows
He had the heart and desire

But he no longer was quick in step
Or had the gas
So Dad turned him out
On the plains of grass

He knew when cows were going
To be moved and worked
Around the barn,
He wandered and lurked

As we would ride off he would run the fence,
Stop and paw at the ground
Although we were mounted,
His replacement had not been found

Twenty years have passed
Since Buck left our place
I catch myself looking in the pasture,
Thinking I'll see him running with grace

Many have come and gone,
But we have yet to have the luck
To be blessed with another family member
Like ol' Buck

Psalm 20:7

LISTENING TO CHRIS

My dear ol' dad called one day,
Asked me to come on by
Said he had bought a new one
I needed to give her a try

This meant he bought one cheap
A good one never has a low price
Grabbed my tapes of Chris,
Was sure I would need some advice

Before I hung up,
I asked Dad about his new mare
He said, No need to worry, son,
Y'all will make a good pair

Changed into my old jeans,
Put on a worn-out shirt
No need to be dressed up nice
When you're goanna hit the dirt

Pulled on my hat, then boots,
As my spurs did clink
Transformed into a bronc rider
In just a wink

Fired up my ol' truck
Turned up Chris LeDoux
By the time I got there,
I'd know just what to do

Pulled up to his arena—there she was,
The new one he wanted me to ride
Dad came out of the barn,
His blue heeler at his side

Got out shaking my head
Asked how much he gave for this ugly mare
He said, I got her cheap,
A price that was low and fair

Now this was not my first rodeo,
Cheap ones always ended up here
So I went out to my ol' truck,
Listened to Chris, and grabbed my cowboy gear

Saddle, halter, rein, and chaps,
Nothing did I miss
Sure glad I was ready
After all, I'd been listening to Chris

Got my saddle on her,
Tightened up the cinch
So far she hadn't moved,
She never did even flinch

Time to mount up
On this cheap one dad had found
Like so many times before,
He had to ear her down

He then said, Son, be easy,
As for the reins I did reach
Every time I got on one,
Dad would give his little speech

One foot in a stirrup,
About to climb into the saddle
That's when I heard Dad say,
Wonder how she'll be rounding up cattle

Reins in one hand,
I had a deep seat
Dad spit out her ear,
Then he unhobbled old Ugly's feet

Within a matter of seconds,
I wished I hadn't answered the phone
Remembering Chris singing
Something about a strawberry roan

Old Ugly dropped her head
And broke and bucked
I thought I heard Chris,
He was still blaring from my ol' truck

First jump was bad,
Second was not any better
But I'd been listening to Chris,
I was sure I had what it took to set 'er

She had a duck, a dive,
As the dust filled the arena air
With every single move,
It was like Chris was right there

After she had given it her all,
She began to smooth out
Heard Dad say, Knew she'd be a good one,
I never had any doubt

You see, Dad didn't have any books
Or videos on how to break a horse
He came from the old school
And he had me listening to Chris, of course

1 John 2:6

THE LITTLE PAINT

When I was young,
A cowboy I wanted to be
Then one day my dad said,
Come to the trailer and see

So I ran from the house,
One boot on, the other in my hand
In that old stock trailer,
A little paint pony did stand

Now a happier little buckaroo
You could not have found anywhere
I now had a paint pony,
And Dad rode a paint mare

Soon I would learn
A more ornery critter God didn't make
The Shetland pony had to be
His only mistake

When eating and being brushed,
He would fool you with his demeanor
Dress him up with bridle and saddle,
There's nothing any meaner

Although kinda short,
That pony on our land,
Dad said, You better cowboy up
And make a hand

Now for his gait,
There was much to be said
I would bounce along
With a bobbling head

Then there was the reining
That left much to be desired
As I pulled and jerked
Till I was worn out and tired

On the ride back to the barn,
He seemed to have a faster stride
A feed bucket waiting on him
Made for a speedy ride

Not listening to cries from me
To stop or slow
Little paint would duck and dive
On the ground I would go

Yes, it was then that I was thankful
For the bellering of the herd
That little paint pony taught me
To use more than one bad word

He would stand there,
Let out a horse laugh with a smile
Knowing I had to mount back up,
For the trip back to the barn was still over a mile

I kept that paint pony
Till him I could no longer stand
A man down the road showed up
Put some cash in my hand

It was then I found out
Just what he was worth
Thirty-five dollars for that pony,
Fifty for saddle and girth

I am now older and look back
With fond memories of that paint pony I once had
The many miles I spent bouncing alongside a paint mare,
The one that carried my dad

John 3:16

BROKEN

There he stood as if chiseled in stone with nostrils flaring
With a stance that seemed to say, Who will be so daring

Who would climb upon his back and try to ride
This mighty steed of such power and kingly pride

For one could see he was master of the brood
He offered protection, and capture had been his to elude

After days of pursuit in the land where only outlaws dwell
He had now been driven into his own living hell

A pen, a corral, or it could be considered a cage
For he had now lost his freedom; it did cause him to rage

So there he stood with nostrils still flaring
Waiting to see who would be so daring

Arrogance and pride could be felt in the mist of the air
Time to mount up, accept the challenge, and victory to declare

As the battle raged with neither willing to give in
The question now was who would break first and who would win

The fight had begun with the object of pride to destroy
One limped away with head dropped, not horse but cowboy

Not all can be broken or are meant to ride
When you mount up, take the reins and swallow your pride

With eyes closed, picturing how the day did unfold
Had he been wrong to be so brash and bold?

There sitting on a split rail as the sun fell and passed away
The cowboy thought, He's not that rank; I just had a bad day

Proverbs 16:18

ONE BAD BUCKAROO

There he stands in cowboy boots and hat,
Cowboy from head to toe
A bowlegged stance
A city slicker would even know

His hand is never empty
It always has a rope
Then there is his smell
To be honest, he sure could use some soap

On his trips to town,
His hips do carry a gun
When most see him coming,
Well, they turn and run

For some reason the rules to him
Seem not to apply
To be honest,
He is not treated like some ordinary guy

One moment he is cowboy charming,
Next he's in a rage
As for his temper,
Well, few know how to gauge

Then there are his sleeping habits,
Up all night and asleep till noon
All of those around him
Are hoping this will be changing pretty soon

He never wants to work
Leaves everything in disarray
Sometimes he's pretty quiet,
With very little to say

When he does speak
All do stop and give an ear
Seems like this cowboy
All wanted to hear

His actions do most of his talking
If you'll just watch and learn
Seems he encounters trouble
Around every corner that he does turn

Now, about this cowboy,
Everyone would agree
He loves every horse, cow, and dog
That he does see

Sometimes it's hard to understand
How around this cowboy one could live
Seems that he wants to take more
Than he is willing to give

That's how life is,
Living with one sure 'nuff bad buckaroo
He rides off on his stick horse
Because his age is only two

Proverbs 22:6

THE UNHAPPY TRAIL

We all gathered there to hear from the trail boss
About driving the herd that was branded with the cross

He said, Boys, are you ready for this cattle drive?
To be honest, some here won't come back alive

Not all are riding for my heavenly brand
There is more to pushing cows and being a top hand

I didn't listen as he warned about what was up ahead
Being a rounder, no way I'd end up dead

As we started out at the break of day
Now was time to show him I knew the cowboy way

Riding on up ahead to find a better trail
What I discovered was a cowboy's hell

All I saw was a desert and cactus all around
As for green grass and water, none could be found

That's when he rode up, said, Cowboy, you are lost
You can ride with me; your soul will be the cost

I didn't know this cowboy, but I accepted his invite
Started riding with him without putting up a fight

We rode into a valley, scorching hot and really deep
Death was all around as I began to sob and weep

He said, Here you'll ride forever, in this hellish land
You didn't listen to the Boss and his great command

I cried out, I want to ride the other way
He said, Cowboy, you should have decided that yesterday

2 Corinthians 6:2

PARDNERS FOR ETERNAL LIFE

We'd been pardners for many years
Rode up on a preacher; he brought me to tears

Told me I was lost, needed to repent
Said Jesus paid it all and was heaven-sent

Stepped off my horse as my pardner watched in disbelief
Got up from my knees, saved; what a relief

Preacher took my hand, led me to the river
My pardner said, Hurry, we have cattle to deliver

As I was going under I could hear my pardner cussing me
Said, Preacher, it won't last, just wait and see

Walked back to my horse, water squishing in my boots
My pardner said, Now you're one of those old coots

I thanked the preacher, said, I'll see you on the other side
Me and my pardner have a long way to ride

As the sun began to warm me and my clothes did dry
My pardner said, Tell the truth; I will know if you lie

This is a joke; you're not really buying this "Jesus thing"
At that very moment, I thought I heard an angel sing

My heart was filled, said, Pardner, I don't mean to boast
But it's not a "Jesus thing," and I have the Holy Ghost

We made it to a town the very next day
I was pretty happy, still had some leftover pay

My pardner said, Come on, let's hit the swinging doors
Said, I'm sorry, but I need to go look in another store

He asked what a store had that I would need
I smiled and said, A Bible so I can read

He threw his hat down, told me I'd lost my mind
Stomped off in a fit, said a new pardner I would have to find

I shouted as he walked out of sight,
Hate you feel that way, but for the first time you're right

Then it hit me—I'd not have to look far
That preacher said Jesus was my bright and morning star

He would guide the way for me down the trail
As I met other cowboys, about him I would tell

Matthew 10:22

SPRING CLEANING

The Boss came riding up
Slid him to a stop
Stepped off like a champ
As every jaw did drop

He then looked around
Didn't recognize their faces
Said, This is my Father's spread
What have you done to his place?

I know I've been gone a while
But this ain't going to get it, hoss
Until Dad says different
I'm still the Boss

This ranch has a purpose
That's why he settled here
If you're not working for him
You need to pack your gear

Then one of them spoke up
Said, We are here to buy and trade
And there's only one of you
We're really not afraid

He then dropped his reins
Grabbed a whip from his saddle
With anger in his voice
Shouted, I'm not driving cattle

The crack of that bullwhip
Sounded like a gun
None wanted to fight
They all were on the run

When the dust died down
He was still standing there
Looking at all of us
Said, This Ranch is for prayer

Picking up the ranch sign
He then nailed it back in place
There on a tree
It simply read, Grace

The Boss then told us, Boys,
To this ranch I have the keys
Every cowboy needs a place
To spend some time on his knees

When I'm not around
Come to my Father's place
You can talk to Him
Like it's face to face

Matthew 21:13

THE RANCH

They rode up to the rancher,
Said, I've heard about this spread
Told my buddy D
He can't have that many a' head

We rode in open pastures
And through a babbling brook
Over a thousand hills
To give this place a look

I will admit this place
Is like nothing I've ever seen
Never in my life
Have I seen grass that tall and green

Then he sat back in his saddle
Wiped the sweat from his brow
The ranch hands went riding past
They had gathered up another cow

Looking at the herd
Said, This isn't what I had in mind
I don't see any registered cows
They're cattle of every kind

Then he began to laugh
Said, I'm a lawyer by trade
I've read about ranching
Good thing I've come to your aid

That's when the Boss spoke up
Replied, I'll give you some advice
This here is my Father's herd
I'm the one that paid the price

You may know the law
Better leave ranching to me
When it come to these cows
There is something you can't see

For your vision is blurred
And I'll tell you why
You're running down my herd
But you have something in your eye

Judging another man's herd
Is simply not your place
You may know the law
But you really have no case

This is my Father's herd
He knows them very well
For what it's worth
None of them are for sell

They might not look like much to you
But Dad knows 'em all by name
They're registered in his book
And in them there is no shame

Matthew 7:1–3

THE STRAY

He had been born out in the brushy land
Raised on not much more than cactus and sand

Tough and mean were just part of his ways
In the desert land that's what it takes to live out your days

We had gathered him up and put him with the herd
All the way he was bellering a little lost cow word

As we drove the herd, he tried to go astray
He never left our sight; that's how we earn our pay

When we got to the corral, he ducked hard at the gate
My pony dropped his head and pushed him in, knowing his fate

As we began to cut out the ones that already had burnt hide
I saw that stray in among them; he had a bullish pride

Then the Boss showed up, said, Boys, time to burn some hair
Pointing at the stray, he shouted, You can start right there

As we rode toward him, he shook his horns to rebel
But I built a loop and swung; through the dusty air it sailed

Jerked my slack and dallied, pulled him out for my pard'
Let out a laugh; his old hide was about to be charred

We had him roped and strung out to take the brand
The Boss was going to him, hot iron in his hand

There in the dirt he was putting up a hellish fight
Yelled out to my pardner, You better stretch him tight

When the Boss got to him, he reached out a hand
Then he touched that stray and he just laid there in the sand

The Boss said, Little stray, you now belong to me
You're now branded with the cross for the whole world to see

I rode in on him to put some slack in my rope
He became part of the Three Cross Ranch—Mercy, Love, and
Hope

Mark 2:4–5

THE CULL

As they looked over the string, one pony stood out
Not because of his strengths; he was anything but stout

The cowboys began to joke about his size and build
One said, He's not worth a bullet or he would be killed

Then he came riding up, the cowboy all knew as J. C.
Said, My Father sent me to have a look and see

We're going to gather our herd, need some strong mounts
Ones that will not weaken when it really counts

I'm not looking for papers or even their bloodline
Just need to find the ones that can hold a fighter on a twine

As he looked them over, said, I'm looking at their hearts
Then he pointed and said, That's where I'll start

The cowboys all looked to see which pony he'd chosen
Then all around the pen, noise and laughter arose

They could not believe; it was the cull he was pointing at
As he pushed back his spotless white cowboy hat

Now boys, you can laugh, but he's the best horse in this herd
He will be a champ; trust me, take my word

So they cut the cull from the herd, laughing all the way
Then J. C. rode over to find out the price he would pay

One of them asked, What will you give for this here cull?
J. C. sat there in the saddle as in his mind he did mull

Then he stepped off his horse that was colored blood red
This horse was a beauty, strong and well bred

He said, I'll trade you straight up, the cull for this here stud
My Father sent me for the cull, and I'll pay for him in blood

Romans 5:8

IN THE STILL OF THE NIGHT

I was riding hard, choking on the dust
My pony beneath me had all of my trust

He was sure-footed and I'd trained him well
Simply the best cow pony, never would be for sell

The day was dragging on as the heat was beating down
I noticed none of the other cowboys were to be found

I was alone there trying to gather the herd
Pushing my pony; he had to be whipped and spurred

Night began to fall and darkness filled the sky
I reached for my canteen but it was bone dry

Weak, hungry, and thirsty, in need of some rest
My pony and I were put to the test

There in the dark I fell to the desert floor
My pony stood still; neither of us could take any more

The herd was calm and all standing still
The darkness brought on the night's cold chill

With no place to turn I fell on my face
Cried out to the Lord, Get me out of this place

As I cried out, he appeared out of the night
To be honest, this cowboy was a heavenly sight

I left the herd as he led me and my pony across the sand
When we reached the camp, I could barely stand

Looking up I said Lord thanks for being my guide
You truly saved this cowboys sorry hide

Then I saw why the other cowboys were of no use
It was plain to see they'd been in the ruckus juice

One of them looked at me and chuckled with a grin,
Glad you made it to the camp; why don't you come on in

That's when the sky rumbled and there came a rushing wind
I knew who it was, my new best friend

The cowboy dropped his jug and jumped to his feet
The fire was blown out; the camp went cold without its heat

All of the cowboys stood there as still as could be
When my friend rode up for all of them to see

He looked at me and said, In heaven waits your reward
For among this bunch you have called me Lord

Psalm 46

COWBOY PAUL

There on the trail the sun was shining bright
His pulled his cowboy hat down but still lost his sight

Falling from his saddle, brought down to his knees
He shouted out, Someone help me, please

The foreman of the Ranch knew he was in distress
Said, Boys, I'll be back; this cowboy I will bless

Then he rode up, said, Cowboy, for me you will ride
I can use you now that I've broken your pride

Paul looked up with joy in his heart
Not knowing what to do or where he would start

For years he had ridden for the other brand
Scattering this man's cattle all across the land

He had cut off his water, set his fields on fire
Had torn down fences when they had stretched wire

Now the righteous cowboy who he had tried to kill
Would give him a new home, a mansion on a hill

At first the other cowboys didn't welcome him in
But in the old corral he proved he rode to win

One day the foreman said, Time to push them west
Paul, you'll be the ramrod at cowboying; you're the best

Early one morning they drove the cattle off their land
Not far into the drive they were jumped by the other brand

The other cowboys, like the cattle, were scattered and set free
But Cowboy Paul was fitted with a noose and taken to a tree

His old boss came riding up on a horse as dark as night
Cowboy Paul sat there, never putting up a fight

They stretched the rope tight and tied it to the tree
As the rustlers gathered around, all wanting to see

His old boss said, Paul, why are you not afraid to die?
Tell me the truth; I'll know if you lie

Cowboy Paul said, Devil, it's plain for all to see
I can do all things through the one that strengthens me

I've ridden for both brands, yours way too long
The brand I'm now ridin' for has made this cowboy strong

You may take my life, but my foreman is by my side
When I leave this world, on heaven's ranch I'll ride

Philippians 4:13

THE OUTLAWS

Once a lawman and one of the best
He hunted down outlaws with zeal and zest

Holding court with the law on his side
Outlaws could run but could never hide

When he caught them, there was no trial
That was simply not this lawman's style

All were guilty who stood before him
They ended up hanging from a tree limb

Then one day on the trail he lost his sight
It was then he finally saw the light

Now he was part of the outlaw horde
Building a mighty ranch for his Lord

Riding across the plains, gathering a herd
Along the way spreading the outlaw word

All the lawmen met one day to make a plan
They were out to get him and all of his clan

They wanted to silence the word he spread
His poster simply said, Wanted Dead

Then the day came when he was caught at last
One said, You know what's coming because of your past

You once were the greatest lawman the world had seen
Now part of the wild bunch, riding on pastures that are green

They read out the warrant, its accusations all lies
Then one turned to him, said, You must surely die

The head lawman said, When you're gone, we will reign
The outlaw replied, For to me to live is Christ, and to die is gain

Philippians 1:21

THE LITTLE MARE

When he walked into the barn
She stood there in her stall
Not the best-looking mare
Her frame a bit too small

While he brushed her
She never moved an inch
Calm as she could be
Nothing made her flinch

As he reached down
And lifted her hoof
She could be trusted
Her past was the proof

Anyone could see
She loved this cowhand
He was her owner
You could tell by the brand

This mare had been wild
Running free on the plains
Not knowing about a saddle
Bridle or reins

Then captured in a corral
One dark and hellish night
Bucking and kicking
She put up an awful fight

At first it appeared
She would be put down
Then a king came riding up
A cowboy hat was his crown

He bought her for a price
One out of love
This kingly cowboy
Had been sent from above

From that day on
The mare never put up a fight
For her cowboy
Was a heavenly sight

He had saved her life
And given her a new home
On his green pastures
She was free to roam

When she was turned out
Free to run and graze
The mare was the object
Of the cowboy's praise

Proverbs 31:30

TOP HAND

We were in the bunkhouse
Resting from the day
Had been up before sunrise
That's how a cowboy earns his pay

All were dead tired
Ready for the night
That rooster would be crowing
Before the morning light

Time for some shut-eye
Some had started to snore
That's when Nighthawk
Came bustin' through the door

Shouted, Boys, get 'em saddled
Rustlers are out tonight
Be sure you're packing
We're in for a fight

We looked like a whirlwind
Grabbing guns and gear
Nighthawk still a-shouting,
Let's get on out of here

We were all surprised
When we got to the herd
The Boss was already there
Said, Boys, I have a word

He said, Now boys,
Y'all are working for me
This herd won't be lost
That's how it's going to be

When they come riding in
You just stand your ground
A better bunch of punchers
I've never found

You all need to know
On this ranch I reign
I can tell you, boys,
Your work is not in vain

Then we saw the rustlers
Riding off of the Triple Cross
They could not get the herd
Because we're riding with the Boss

1 Corinthians 15:58

COWBOY PROVERBS

A good friend is like a good pair of boots: hard to find and worth the price, and you never want to get rid of them. "A friend loveth at all times" (Prov. 17:17).

Sitting in the emergency room is like sitting in church. Everyone has a problem; some are just easier to see. "When Jesus heard it, he saith unto them, They that are whole have no need of the physician, but they that are sick: I came not to call the righteous, but sinners to repentance" (Mark 2:17).

Arguing with a lost person is like branding ducks. You can do it, but what's the point? You'll just burn them and they'll still head south. "Let your speech be always with grace, seasoned with salt, that ye may know how ye ought to answer every man" (Col. 4:6).

I do not have short-man syndrome. I have vertically challenged disorder.

Arrogance is confidence without ability.

Be careful when shoving something down someone's throat. You can get bitten. "A brother offended is harder to be won than a strong city: and their contentions are like the bars of a castle" (Ps. 18:19).

My dreams turned into a nightmare, my nightmare turned into reality, and my reality turned into my life. My life turned to Jesus, Jesus changed my reality, and his reality has no nightmares. Now I am living the life he has for me, and it is better than a dream.

Sharing your faith in Christ is like riding a bucking horse. Sometimes you get bucked off, but it is still a great ride. And you will never be bucked off if you never get on. "So then faith cometh by hearing, and hearing by the word of God" (Rom. 10:17).

My horse has to be faster than the stampede and sure-footed where there is no trail. During troubled times, you want to be confident in the one that is carrying you. "Hear my cry, O God; attend unto my prayer. From the end of the earth will I cry unto thee, when my heart is overwhelmed: lead me to the rock that is higher than I" (Ps. 61:1–2).

Having false hope is like riding a saddle with dry-rotted latigos. It will hold you up for a while, but under stress it will break. Ride with confidence in Christ. "The LORD is my rock, and my fortress, and my deliverer; my God, my strength, in whom I will trust; my buckler, and the horn of my salvation, and my high tower" (Ps. 18:2).

If a horse kicks you, it is because it is his nature. If a Christian kicks you, it is because of his old nature. Your actions show which nature you are following. "Therefore if any man be in Christ, he is a new creature: old things are passed away; behold, all things are become new" (2 Cor. 5:17).

Life is too short to ride a sorry horse.

Rusty rowels and a dusty Bible happen for the same reason—not being used!

If you bought the horse, don't complain about how he rides.

Wearing boots that are too small is like having unconfessed sin. Your walk might look normal, but you know the pain you are in. 1 John 1:9 If we confess our sins, he is faithful and just to forgive us our sins, and to cleanse us from all unrighteousness.

My dad never bought a good horse. However, he did buy several sorry ones and work with them. "For all have sinned, and come short of the glory of God" (Rom. 3:23).

If you whip a dead horse long enough, all you'll get is a sore arm and flies hanging around you. And you'll still be in the same place. At some point you have to move on. "Every way of a man is right in his own eyes: but the LORD pondereth the hearts" (Prov. 21:2).

You don't have to play the cards that life has dealt you. You can fold and move on to another game. Often people choose to play the same old losing hand. "For whosoever shall call upon the name of the Lord shall be saved" (Rom. 10:13).

As Christian cowboys and cowgirls, we are to gather up the strays and let the Lord brand and dehorn them!

A worn-out horse will never catch a cow, and eventually everyone will just think you have a sorry horse. Likewise, a worn-out Christian will not be effective, and eventually everyone will just think you're a sorry Christian. "And God blessed the seventh day, and sanctified it: because that in it he had rested from all his work which God created and made" (Gen. 2:3).

You load your horse in the trailer to take it where you want to go. If your horse is hard to load, you often are late or miss out on what was planned. When we load up, so to speak, with Christ, we are to go where he wants us to go. "I beseech you therefore, brethren, by the mercies of God, that ye present your bodies a living sacrifice, holy, acceptable unto God, which is your reasonable service" (Rom. 12:1).

An empty feed bucket is like empty preaching that does not call for change in your walk. It may bring them to the pen, but it doesn't provide what is needed for growth. "Wherefore laying aside all malice, and all guile, and hypocrisies, and envies, and all evil speakings, as newborn babes, desire the sincere milk of the word, that ye may grow thereby" (1 Peter 2:1–2).

If you never saddle your horse and mount up, you will not get far down the trail. "But be ye doers of the word, and not hearers only, deceiving your own selves" (James 1:22).

You can ride without cinching your saddle tight. However, when the trail gets tough or you head down into the valley, odds are you're going to hit the ground. As Christians, we are to be close to the Lord so that when the trail gets tough, we don't fall. "Draw nigh to God, and he will draw nigh to you" (James 4:8).

What do a bucking horse, a roping horse, and a ranch horse have in common? They are all horses, and a good one makes the owner look good. The same is true of a Christian's spiritual gift. "And he gave some, apostles; and some, prophets; and some, evangelists; and some, pastors and teachers; for the perfecting of the saints, for the work of the ministry, for the edifying of the body of Christ" (Eph. 4:11–12).

If your horse is taking you down the wrong trail, it's not his fault; you're the one with the reins in your hands. If your life is going down the wrong trail, check and see whose hands the reins are in—yours or the Lord's. "He restoreth my soul: he leadeth me in the paths of righteousness for his name's sake" (Ps. 23:3).

You cannot catch one if you never build a loop. You cannot lead someone to Christ if you never share your faith. "So then faith cometh by hearing, and hearing by the word of God" (Rom. 10:17).

If one type of bit worked on every horse, there would be just one. Jesus is not against the traditional church, contemporary church, or cowboy church. He is against the dead-complacent church! A church is only as alive as its members. "I know thy works, that thou art neither cold nor hot: I would thou wert cold or hot. So then because thou art lukewarm, and neither cold nor hot, I will spue thee out of my mouth" (Rev. 3:15–16).

From roping to racing, you will never win on an unhealthy, out-of-shape horse. And if you do win, it is because the other horses are in worse shape than yours. A spiritually unhealthy and out-of-shape Christian is a defeated Christian. We need to be confessed up, prayed up, and in the word to have victory every day. "I have fought a good fight, I have finished my course, I have kept the faith" (2 Tim. 4:7).

If a cow pony has never followed a cow, is it really a cow pony? If a "Christian" never follows Christ, is he or she really a Christian? "And he saith unto them, Follow me, and I will make you fishers of men" (Matt. 4:19).

You can put a saddle and bridle on a goat, but that does not make it a horse. "Not every one that saith unto me, Lord, Lord, shall enter into the kingdom of heaven; but he that doeth the will of my Father which is in heaven" (Matt. 7:21).

The difference in a good horse and a good friend is that a good horse will carry you over a rocky trail because it's been trained to, but a good friend will carry you during a rocky time because he or she wants to. "A man that hath friends must shew himself friendly: and there is a friend that sticketh closer than a brother" (Prov. 18:24).

If life is too hard to handle, check to see what you are holding on to. "Trust in the LORD with all thine heart; and lean not unto thine own understanding. In all thy ways acknowledge him, and he shall direct thy paths" (Prov. 3:5–6).

Life is like a Shetland pony—short, a rough ride, and mean at times but still a great gift from God. "My brethren, count it all joy when ye fall into divers temptations; Knowing this, that the trying of your faith worketh patience" (James 1:2–3).

A good horse trainer can take any horse and make it useful for something. Regardless of its papers, it is still just a horse. Regardless of your "papers," God can and will save you and make you useful for kingdom work. "But ye shall receive power, after that the Holy Ghost is come upon you: and ye shall be witnesses unto me" (Acts 1:8).

If your horse throws you off, get up and get back on. If he throws you every time, get a new horse. Not everything in our walk is from the Lord; some is there because of choices we made. "Let no man say when he is tempted, I am tempted of

God: for God cannot be tempted with evil, neither tempteth he any man: But every man is tempted, when he is drawn away of his own lust, and enticed" (James 1:13–14).

If your horse stumbles, you are thankful that he gathered himself, pat his neck, and continue on your ride. If a brother stumbles, we often get out of the way and watch him fall. "Brethren, if a man be overtaken in a fault, ye which are spiritual, restore such an one in the spirit of meekness; considering thyself, lest thou also be tempted. Bear ye one another's burdens, and so fulfil the law of Christ" (Gal. 6:1–2).

It does not matter that you are riding the fastest horse around. If you take the wrong trail, you're just the first one lost. "Enter through the narrow gate; for the gate is wide and the way is broad that leads to destruction, and there are many who enter through it" (Matt. 7:13).

You can ride a saddle that does not fit on a trail drive and reach the end of the trail. But the ride is uncomfortable and you let some cattle get by you because you are just holding on. If you are not growing in the fruit of the spirit, the result is the same. "But the fruit of the Spirit is love, joy, peace, longsuffering, gentleness, goodness, faith, meekness, temperance: against such there is no law. And they that are Christ's have crucified the flesh with the affections and lusts. If we live in the Spirit, let us also walk in the Spirit" (Gal. 5:22–25).

There's nothing wrong with getting thrown; just don't blame your horse if you can't ride. "The way of a fool is right in his own eyes: but he that hearkeneth unto counsel is wise" (Prov. 12:15).

Putting your saddle on backward and riding it that way is like the way we handle our "secret" sins: we think no one will notice. But the entire time, the Lord and most around us know we are headed in the wrong direction. "Let not sin therefore reign in your mortal body, that ye should obey it in the lusts thereof" (Rom. 6:12).

Marriage is like a good cowboy hat. It fits even better after it has been through a few storms if you'll keep wearing it and not trade it in for a new one. "Therefore shall a man leave his father and his mother, and shall cleave unto his wife: and they shall be one flesh" (Gen. 2:24).

It's not always the best-looking horse that wins the race! "Judge not, and ye shall not be judged: condemn not, and ye shall not be condemned: forgive, and ye shall be forgiven" (Luke 6:37).

Before you tell someone how sorry his cow is, you'd better inspect your whole herd. "And why beholdest thou the mote that is in thy brother's eye, but perceivest not the beam that is in thine own eye?" (Luke 6:41).

Holding a grudge is like wrestling a skunk. You can do it, but odds are that you'll end up being the one who stinks and who no one wants to be around. "And be ye kind one to another, tenderhearted, forgiving one another, even as God for Christ's sake hath forgiven you" (Eph. 4:32).

Tragedy is not drawing a sorry bronc you can't win on. Tragedy is not being entered in the rodeo when someone is willing to pay your fees. "Behold, I stand at the door, and knock: if any man hear my voice, and open the door, I will come in to him, and will sup with him, and he with me" (Rev. 3:20).

It doesn't matter how good your cows are if you have a sorry bull! What we are attached to is what we produce. "For a good tree bringeth not forth corrupt fruit; neither doth a corrupt tree bring forth good fruit. For every tree is known by his own fruit. For of thorns men do not gather figs, nor of a bramble bush gather they grapes" (Luke 6:43–44).

Not everyone on the trail is riding the same direction. "Blessed is the man that walketh not in the counsel of the ungodly, nor standeth in the way of sinners, nor sitteth in the seat of the scornful. But his delight is in the law of the LORD; and in his law doth he meditate day and night" (Ps. 1:1–2).

The more time you spend in the saddle, the better acquainted with your horse you become. In the process, you become a better cowboy or cowgirl. "Not forsaking the assembling of ourselves together, as the manner of some is; but exhorting one another: and so much the more, as ye see the day approaching" (Heb. 10:25).

I have never heard a horse moo! "… for out of the abundance of the heart the mouth speaketh" (Matt. 12:34).

Blowing your own horn plays to deaf ears.

If you follow the wrong trail boss, not only will the herd be lost but you will be as well. "Beloved, believe not every spirit, but try the spirits whether they are of God: because many false prophets are gone out into the world" (1 John 4:1).

The thing about a pity party is that everyone is invited but you're the only one who shows up!

Breaking the spirit of a horse does not mean you have made it obedient. Submitting to the Lord is obedience and brings about a new spirit. "Create in me a clean heart, O God; and renew a right spirit within me" (Ps. 51:10).

If you have to question the trail you're taking, you already have the answer. "All things are lawful for me, but all things are not expedient: all things are lawful for me, but all things edify not" (1 Cor. 10:23).

If you're right all the time, you are running with a pretty ignorant crowd. "Every way of a man is right in his own eyes: but the LORD pondereth the hearts" (Prov. 21:2).

The thing about eating crow is that no matter how you prepare it, it's still crow! "Whoso keepeth his mouth and his tongue keepeth his soul from troubles" (Prov. 21:23).

I still have my first pair of cowboy boots and first belt and buckle. They no longer fit. If I still wanted to wear them, there would be a problem. If I could still wear them, there would be a bigger problem. "When I was a child, I spake as a child, I understood as a child, I thought as a child: but when I became a man, I put away childish things" (1 Cor. 13:11).

Don't get mad at a green broke horse that acts like a green broke horse; it just needs a little more schooling. "Brethren, if a man be overtaken in a fault, ye which are spiritual, restore such an one in the spirit of meekness; considering thyself, lest thou also be tempted" (Gal. 6:1).

At the end of the trail is not when you want to realize you took a wrong turn. "For it is written, As I live, saith the Lord, every knee shall bow to me, and every tongue shall confess to God. So then every one of us shall give account of himself to God" (Rom. 14:11–12).

If your corral is empty, don't blame the cows; they will stay in the pasture until you round them up. After all, that's what cows do! "And the lord said unto the servant, Go out into the highways and hedges, and compel them to come in, that my house may be filled" (Luke 14:23).

It's not how many times you get bucked off that matters; it's how many times you get back on. "For a just man falleth seven times, and riseth up again: but the wicked shall fall into mischief" (Prov. 24:16).

If you have to tell everyone how good of a cowboy you are, you're not much of one. "Whoso boasteth himself of a false gift is like clouds and wind without rain" (Prov. 25:14).

My politics do not determine my faith; my faith determines my politics. "When the righteous are in authority, the people rejoice: but when the wicked beareth rule, the people mourn" (Prov. 29:2).

Just because something draws a big crowd does not mean it is of the Lord. I've been around cattle enough to know that flies will gather around stuff that's not worth eating. "Beware lest any man spoil you through philosophy and vain deceit, after the tradition of men, after the rudiments of the world, and not after Christ" (Col. 2:8).

Some might say I am complex, a contradiction, and confused. I prefer simple, sure, and saved.

Just because I am a simple man doesn't mean I am simpleminded.

Sometimes our horses come up lame on the trail of life so we can realize we are headed in the wrong direction. "Be still, and know that I am God: I will be exalted among the heathen, I will be exalted in the earth" (Ps. 46:10).

I feel like I'm living life in the fast lane but in an old, worn-out Ford Pinto.

If your horse kicks you, your dog bites you, a steer hooks you, the cook hates you, and the bunkhouse has fleas, maybe you're working on the wrong ranch. "And call upon me in the day of trouble: I will deliver thee, and thou shalt glorify me" (Ps. 50:15).

I have met many who have all the answers, but they don't know the questions. "Even so the tongue is a little member, and boasteth great things. Behold, how great a matter a little fire kindleth!" (James 3:5).

When the herd stampedes, you know it was not what the trail boss wanted. "For where envying and strife is, there is confusion and every evil work" (James 3:16).

You can hitch up a sheep with horses to a stagecoach, but it will not last long. At some point, it will get tired and be dragged to death. "Be ye not unequally yoked together with unbelievers: for what fellowship hath righteousness with unrighteousness? and what communion hath light with darkness?" (2 Cor. 6:14).

You can cut hay strings with a dull knife, but it is less of a struggle with a sharp one. You can break free of what has you bound up with little faith and not much knowledge of the word, but it is less of a struggle with a strong faith and understanding of God's word. "For the word of God is quick, and powerful, and sharper than any twoedged sword, piercing even to the dividing asunder of soul and spirit, and of the joints and marrow, and is a discerner of the thoughts and intents of the heart" (Heb. 4:12).

It is easier to crawl through a barbwire fence when you have a friend helping hold the strands apart. You are less likely to get hung up or snagged. We all need people in our lives to help keep us from getting hung up on something. "Where no counsel is, the people fall: but in the multitude of counsellors there is safety" (Prov. 11:14).

Sitting on the fence at the rodeo does not make you a cowboy; it makes you a spectator. There comes a time when you have to enter up and show your skills. Too many Christians are just sitting in pews and not using their gifts. Time to enter up!

If you are gripping the saddle horn with both hands when your horse begins to buck, you will never get him under control. When life starts to buck, you have to turn loose to get control. "Preserve me, O God: for in thee do I put my trust" (Ps. 16:1).

I've learned that living life going wide open empties the tank a lot quicker.

It does not matter how well you rope or ride in the practice pen. Enter up, drive a thousand miles, pay your fees, and then see what you are made of. Anyone can serve and worship the Lord one hour on Sunday morning. How well do you do in the world? "And whosoever doth not bear his cross, and come after me, cannot be my disciple" (Luke 14:27).

When you wean a calf, you do not leave it in the same pasture with its mama; they have to be separated. If not, that calf will return to its mama. Often we are like a weaning calf bawling and bellering for what we do not need. "Knowing this, that our old man is crucified with him, that the body of sin might be destroyed, that henceforth we should not serve sin" (Rom. 6:6).

It's not that most people don't have something to say; it is that most don't have anything to say that's worth listening to. "I will hear what God the LORD will speak: for he will speak peace unto his people, and to his saints: but let them not turn again to folly" (Ps. 85:8).

Friends can be like money—easy to come by but hard to hold on to. But if one invests in them wisely, he will see long-range dividends.

After you ear tag your cows for flies, they still have to swat some with their tails. After you get saved, you still have to swat the temptation that comes along. "Submit yourselves therefore to God. Resist the devil, and he will flee from you" (James 4:7).

If you are going to lay it all on the line, make sure the line is strong enough to handle it.

When you live your life as an open book, don't be surprised if some people don't like some of the chapters.

The trail I'm riding on has rocks, snakes, and cactus all around. As long as I'm still in the saddle, they have no effect on me. It is when I step off and start walking on my own that I stumble, get bitten, and fall into something that hurts. "And the LORD shall help them, and deliver them: he shall deliver them from the wicked, and save them, because they trust in him" (Ps. 37:40).

Having a Bible you never read is like leading your horse around in the wilderness. It can't take you where you need to go if you never mount up. "So then faith cometh by hearing, and hearing by the word of God" (Rom. 10:17).

If you get to the rodeo and find your trailer is empty, don't blame your horse; he will not load himself. If your church is empty, don't blame the lost. "But if our gospel be hid, it is hid to them that are lost" (2 Cor. 4:3).

If you can no longer reach the stirrups and cannot get on your horse, you need one of two things: a shorter horse or better friends who will give you a hand. "If a brother or sister be naked, and destitute of daily food, and one of you say unto them, Depart in peace, be ye warmed and filled; notwithstanding ye give them not those things which are needful to the body; what doeth it profit?" (James 2:15–16).

Never trade a good friend for a sorry horse. "A man that hath friends must shew himself friendly: and there is a friend that sticketh closer than a brother" (Prov. 18:24).

Even a drugstore cowboy can drive a herd when things are calm. But when the storm hits, lightning flashes, and the stampede begins, that is when you find out who is just wearing a hat. "Though I walk in the midst of trouble, thou wilt revive me: thou shalt stretch forth thine hand against the wrath of mine enemies, and thy right hand shall save me" (Ps. 138:7).

The difference between being brave and being stupid is the outcome.

Dad taught me to hold on to the reins when I hit the ground. If I didn't, it would be a long walk home. "If thou faint in the day of adversity, thy strength is small" (Prov. 24:10).

I remember the first time I helped Dad pull a calf; I learned a lot about life right there. That calf was going to die without help. We had to get a little messy, but its life was saved. "And brought them out, and said, Sirs, what must I do to be saved? And they said, Believe on the Lord Jesus Christ, and thou shalt be saved, and thy house" (Acts 16:30–31).

A horse that is turned out to pasture can feel two ways: free or abandoned. "Two are better than one; because they have a good reward for their labour" (Ecc. 4:9).

When I was a kid, I had a Shetland pony. He was fat, mean, and rough riding. One thing about him, though—no matter how far you rode him, he still knew his way back to the barn and the feed trough. No matter how far away you have gotten, the Lord is waiting for you to return. "If we confess our sins, he is faithful and just to forgive us of our sin and cleanse us from all unrighteousness" (1 John 1:9).

When the rodeo announcer says, "Better luck next time, cowboy," you know you will have a chance to enter another rodeo and try again. You only get one chance, though, to stand before the Lord and hear, "Well done, thou good and faithful servant."

Being cowboy tough means you don't have insurance or the money to go to the hospital! "A merry heart doeth good like a medicine: but a broken spirit drieth the bones" (Prov. 17:22).

It doesn't matter if you have the best roping horse, barrel horse, or dogging horse; if you never load him up and enter, he is not worth much. You can be the most gifted person on earth, but if you never use that gift to glorify the Lord, it's not worth much. "Neglect not the gift that is in thee" (1 Tim. 4:14).

Your buckle may say "World Champion"; mine says "State Champion," and someone else's might not say anything. But in the end, they all do the same thing—hold your pants up. "And if ye call on the Father, who without respect of persons judgeth according to every man's work, pass the time of your sojourning here in fear" (1 Peter 1:17).

When you say you want your life to be a bed of roses, just remember that roses have stickers and fertilizer! "Yet man is born unto trouble, as the sparks fly upward" (Job 5:7).

Until you have scars from it, you really haven't given it your all.

Riding the horse in front of Wal-Mart doesn't make you a cowboy. Any kid with fifty cents and a dirty diaper can do that.

If someone is riding an ugly horse, that's his business. I've read the whole book, and criticism and discouragement are not fruits of the spirit! "But exhort (encourage) one another daily, while it is called To day; lest any of you be hardened through the deceitfulness of sin" (Heb. 3:13).

The best horse my dad ever owned would, from time to time, "forget" that he was broke. "Therefore to him that knoweth to do good, and doeth it not, to him it is sin" (James 4:17).

A goat will eat anything; a sheep will not. What you feed on will determine what you are. Christians are to be sheep! "Blessed are they which do hunger and thirst after righteousness: for they shall be filled" (Matt. 5:6).

To get paid on Friday, you have to saddle up on Monday. I love Mondays; it means the Lord has given me another day to serve him. "Fight the good fight of faith, lay hold on eternal life, whereunto thou art also called, and hast professed a good profession before many witnesses" (1 Tim. 6:12).

A horse that is lathered up may not be overworked; he may just be out of shape. "Confess your faults one to another, and pray one for another, that ye may be healed. The effectual fervent prayer of a righteous man availeth much" (James 5:16).

Having a horse in your pasture does not make you a cowboy, and having a Bible on your bookshelf does not make you a Christian.

A fence is built for several reasons: to keep stuff in, to keep stuff out, to set boundaries, and to separate your herd. The word of God exists for the same reasons. "I will delight myself in thy statutes: I will not forget thy word" (Ps. 119:16).

If you turn out every bull that does not fit you, that is mean, or that you think you can't win any money on, you are going to miss some opportunities to win. You never know when a bull is going to have a good day. If you turn out every friend who is difficult at times or does not see everything the way you do, you will miss their good days and opportunities to make great memories. "But if ye do not forgive, neither will your Father which is in heaven forgive your trespasses" (Mark 11:26).

If you have to buy your friends, remember that they will leave you for the next highest bidder. I have a friend in Jesus who will never leave me nor forsake me, and I was bought by his blood.

Sometimes it's not a burr under your saddle that makes your horse act stupid. It could be the burr in the saddle that is the problem. "A double minded man is unstable in all his ways" (James 1:8).

Friends are like false teeth: good ones put a smile on your face, and bad ones just make you look foolish. "Blessed is the man that walketh not in the counsel of the ungodly, nor standeth in the way of sinners, nor sitteth in the seat of the scornful" (Ps. 1:1).

If you are too ashamed of your horse to unload him at the rodeo, you will never win or even place. Victory comes from letting the one that got you there carry you. "For whosoever shall be ashamed of me and of my words, of him shall the Son of man be ashamed, when he shall come in his own glory, and in his Father's, and of the holy angels" (Luke 9:26).

If you do not like who I am, rest assured that you would have hated who I once was. My happiness is not dependent on your liking me but rather on the Lord's loving me.

Broken promises are like a broken rope. You can tie it back together, but you are always going to wonder when it is going to break again.

I've watched enough westerns to know that it does not matter what kind of gun is carried into battle—pistol, rifle, or shotgun. If it is never fired, the enemy cannot be defeated. The word is our weapon, and it is time to fire a few rounds! "Let the redeemed of the LORD say so, whom he hath redeemed from the hand of the enemy" (Ps. 107:2).

If you always go for broke, don't be surprised if you end up there—broke. "As for God, his way is perfect: the word of the LORD is tried: he is a buckler to all those that trust in him" (Ps. 18:30).

Not everything you get on you in the arena is dirt, but it all washes off. In the arena of life, sometimes we get into things that are more than just dirt. "If we confess our sins, he is faithful and just to forgive us our sins, and to cleanse us from all unrighteousness" (1 John 1:9).

There are three T's that every cowboy needs to know: talent will get you noticed, try will get you respect, and talk will get you nowhere! "Let the words of my mouth, and the meditation of my heart, be acceptable in thy sight, O LORD, my strength, and my redeemer" (Ps. 19:14).

Never trust a man your dog does not like!
Don't waste your time listening to a man with nothing to say. "Excellent speech becometh not a fool: much less do lying lips a prince" (Prov. 17:7).

The difference between being on the wagon and off the wagon is only one step.

You can't circle the wagons in a wagon train of one. "Not forsaking the assembling of ourselves together, as the manner of some is; but exhorting one another: and so much the more, as ye see the day approaching" (Heb. 10:25).

One of the best things about heaven is that there will be no negative people, thoughts, or words there.

If all you ever do is whip your horse, don't be surprised when you discover that you have an empty barn. "By this shall all men know that ye are my disciples, if ye have love one to another" (John 13:35).

The Lone Ranger was not really "lone"—he had a companion, Tonto. We are not the Lone Christians; God has given us a companion, the Holy Spirit. "Nevertheless I tell you the truth; it is expedient for you that I go away: for if I go not away, the Comforter will not come unto you; but if I depart, I will send him unto you" (John 16:7).

You would never expect a horse to shovel out its own stall. It's your job! A new Christian may need to get some things out of his or her life, and it's your job as a mature Christian to help. "But the Comforter, which is the Holy Ghost, whom the Father will send in my name, he shall teach you all things, and bring all things to your remembrance, whatsoever I have said unto you" (John 14:26).

If you don't like my cowboy hat, you're sure not going to like what is on my boots. "Woe unto you, scribes and Pharisees, hypocrites! for ye are like unto whited sepulchres, which indeed appear beautiful outward, but are within full of dead men's bones, and of all uncleanness" (Matt. 23:27).

Mom always said I had a headful of rocks and a heart of stone. Now she is right. "He (the Lord) only is my rock and my salvation: he is my defence; I shall not be moved" (Ps. 62:6).

You can be the world's greatest heeler, but if your header never catches, you're just riding your horse. "Two are better than one; because they have a good reward for their labour. For if they fall, the one will lift up his fellow: but woe to him that is alone when he falleth; for he hath not another to help him up" (Ecc. 4:9–10).

Just because you have a pasture full of horses does not mean you're a great trainer. It could just mean you're a sorry salesman. "Examine yourselves, whether ye be in the faith; prove your own selves. Know ye not your own selves, how that Jesus Christ is in you, except ye be reprobates?" (2 Cor. 13:5).

Always remember that thunder and lighting can stampede the herd. "Do all things without murmurings and disputings: that ye may be blameless and harmless, the sons of God, without rebuke, in the midst of a crooked and perverse nation, among whom ye shine as lights in the world" (Phil. 2:14–15).

If you don't like riding, don't saddle up. "Serve the LORD with gladness: come before his presence with singing" (Ps. 100:2).

When you're going under is not the time to open your mouth but rather to open your heart. "I cried with my whole heart; hear me, O LORD: I will keep thy statutes" (Ps. 119:145).

An unused Bible is like an empty gun: when the thief comes to kill, steal, and destroy, you cannot protect yourself. "Thy word have I hid in mine heart, that I might not sin against thee" (Ps. 119:11).

A stick horse will carry you only as far as you can go. "The horse is prepared against the day of battle: but safety is of the LORD" (Prov. 21:31).

If your cattle are not fed, they become food for the buzzards. A Christian not fed the word becomes food for the devil. "Be sober, be vigilant; because your adversary the devil, as a roaring lion, walketh about, seeking whom he may devour" (1 Peter 5:8).

My old buckle still fits; it's the belt that is giving me trouble.

When you clean out your horse stalls, you have one of two things: a load of something that stinks or fertilizer that helps things grow. It is all in how you look at it and what you do with it. "My brethren, count it all joy when ye fall into divers temptations (trials); knowing this, that the trying of your faith worketh patience" (James 1:2–3).

I've been knocked down enough times in life to know that getting up is easy when you realize you're not dead. "I am crucified with Christ: nevertheless I live; yet not I, but Christ liveth in me: and the life which I now live in the flesh I live by the faith of the Son of God, who loved me, and gave himself for me" (Gal. 2:20).

It's not about who I was but who I am. It's not about where I was but where I am headed. It's not about what I have but what he gave. It's not about me but about Jesus Christ my Lord!

God gives everyone a spiritual gift. It is not to be hidden away in a closet or placed on the mantel to be adored. It is to be shared with the world to bring honor and glory to him.

The difference between a good memory and a bad one is where you keep it stored—in your heart or in your mind.

My past is regrettable. My present is respectable. My future is remarkable.

I once ran with the devil and ran from the Lord. Now I run with the Lord and the devil runs from me. "Submit yourselves therefore to God. Resist the devil, and he will flee from you" (James 4:7).

A man without goals will reach his quickly.

If all you do in life is play games, you're not going to like the final score!

A good friend is like a good horse: he will carry you where you need to go regardless of how rough the trail is.

People who live in glass houses should be in better shape.

A closed fist is not a helping hand.

If you're holding on to the Lord, nothing can hold you back When life has you face down, as you struggle to get up stop at your knees. It gets better from there. "Is any among you afflicted? let him pray. Is any merry? let him sing psalms" (James 5:13).

SADDLE UP WITH JESUS AND GET ON THE TRAIL

Prayer

Jesus, I want to know you; I want you to come into my life so that I can begin following you as the Lord of my life. I'm sorry for the things I've done and admit that I am a sinner separated from you because of sin. I am asking that you forgive me for my sin. Thank you for dying on the cross and paying the price for my sin so that I can have a personal relationship with you. I believe you are the only one who can do this. Only you can give me the power through the Holy Spirit to change and become the person you created me to be. Thank you for forgiving my past mistakes and for giving me eternal life. I give my life to you. Please do with it as you wish. In Jesus' name I ask. Amen.

LaVergne, TN USA
09 November 2010
204072LV00002B/1/P